Tiberius
goes to school

for Henrietta

First published by Tiberius Publishing
The Cottage
8 Kimberley Road
Nuthall
Nottingham NG16 1DG

Written by Keith Harvey
Designed by Kait Brown

First published in 2002

A CIP catalogue record for this title is available from the British Library

Hardback ISBN: 1 902604 04 0
Printed and bound in Spain

Tiberius
goes to school

Written by Keith Harvey

Illustrated by Kait Brown

Tiberius, a little mouse with a long tail and pink ears, popped his nose over the duvet and peeped out.

Then he popped back under again.

‘Do I really have
to get out of bed?’
he thought. ‘It’s so
cosy curled up in here.’

Then he remembered that he did have to get out of bed because he had some jobs to do around the house and a bit of shopping to do in the village.

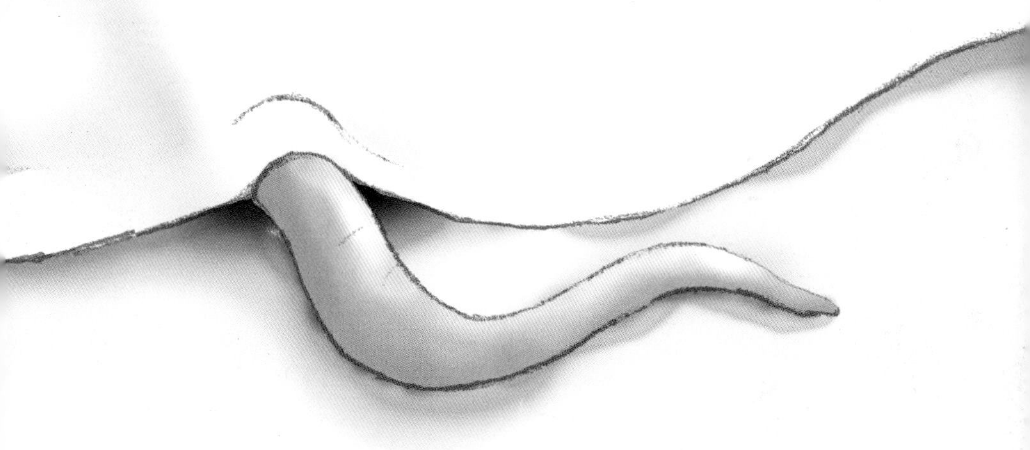

“Oh never mind,” he sighed.
“I’ll have a lie in another day.”

He hopped out of bed and went to have his breakfast. He had a bowl of cheeseflakes. He nearly always had cheeseflakes, although he did occasionally have cheese on toast for a change.

'I think I'll go to the village first to do my shopping, and then when I get back I can concentrate on my jobs around the house.'

He set off and when he reached the signpost he knew which way he was going.

He turned right and went down to the village.

On the way he met Sir Patrick Fitzwarren's daughter, Georgina and her cousin Henrietta.

Georgina and Henrietta told Tiberius that they were on their way to school.

“I’ve never been to school,” said Tiberius.
“Never been to school?” said Henrietta.
“No, never, what’s it like?”

Georgina and Henrietta looked at each other and whispered something.

"We've got an idea," said Henrietta. "Why don't you pop into my pocket when we get to school and I'll smuggle you in?"

"Really?" said Tiberius, "but what will the teacher say?"

"Don't worry," replied Henrietta. "She will never know you are there if you stay in my pocket."

When they arrived at the school gates Tiberius climbed into Henrietta's pocket.

It was a bit dark and sticky inside but Tiberius was too excited to worry much about that.

He found that if he stood on tiptoe he could just see over the top of the pocket, but of course realised that he would have to be very quiet and careful to make sure no-one could see him.

The lessons began and Tiberius kept very still, although he did nibble a few of the crumbs in Henrietta's pocket.

Every now and then he couldn't resist having a little peek out of the pocket.

After a while Tiberius heard the teacher, Miss Merryweather, say that they were going to do some finger painting.

“What’s that?” he whispered to Henrietta.

“You put your fingers instead of a brush into the paint and then paint a pattern or a picture onto the paper with your fingers.”

“That sounds like fun. I wish I could have a go at that,” said Tiberius.

“OK, I’ll let you have a go when the teacher’s not looking,” said Henrietta.

Tiberius popped back inside the pocket with a smile on his face.

He seemed to be waiting for ages and ages.

Then Henrietta suddenly whispered, “Now Tiberius, quickly!”

He clambered out of the pocket and onto the desk, and jumped onto the edge of a bright blue paint pot.

The pot wobbled as he put his hand inside and although he stretched, he couldn’t quite reach the bottom of the pot.

Then something dreadful happened.

Tiberius slipped, PLOP, right into the pot of paint!

“Help, help!” he squeaked as Henrietta pulled him out by his tail.

“You were only supposed to dip your fingers in it,” giggled Georgina.

"I'm so sorry," said Tiberius, "but I'm sure I'll make a good job of the painting now." So with that

he jumped...

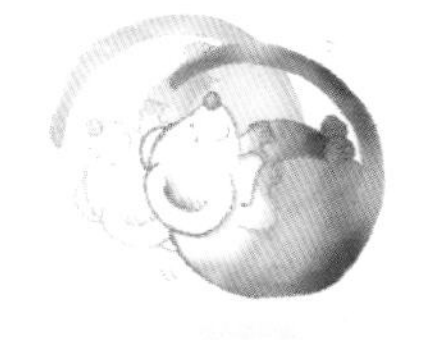

he rolled...

and he walked

all over the paper until almost all of the paint had come off him.

"I think that looks rather good," said Henrietta. "I love your little handprints here and there."

Suddenly Miss Merryweather called out for the children to finish their pictures and bring them over to her.

"Quickly, back in my pocket," said Henrietta, as she stood in line waiting to hand over her picture.

From inside the pocket Tiberius could hear Miss Merryweather talking to the children while they showed her their paintings.

“Well done Rupert... very good Rachel... excellent Sophie and very good Georgina.”

Tiberius knew that Henrietta was next and he wondered what the teacher would say about her picture.

“Henrietta, what’s this and what are these prints here?” Miss Merryweather asked.

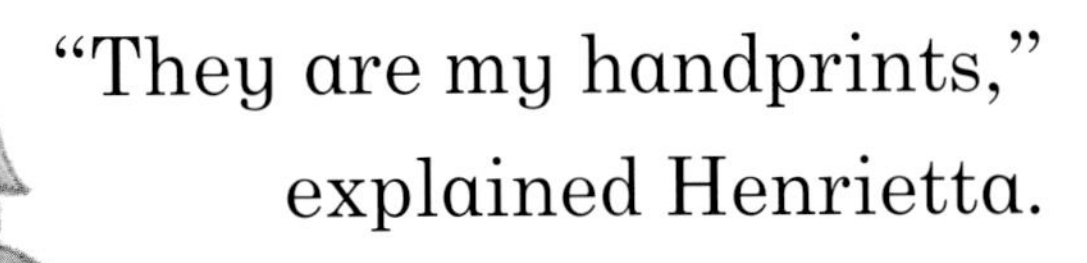

"They are my handprints," explained Henrietta.

"Oh Henrietta they can't be your handprints, your hands are far too big to make such small prints. What have you done?"

'Oh dear,' thought Tiberius. 'This sounds like trouble.'

So, quick as a wink, he jumped out of the pocket and onto Miss Merryweather's desk, thinking that she would understand when he explained what had happened.

In fact, he thought she would be quite amused but Miss Merryweather was most definitely not amused. Her eyes nearly popped out of her head, and as Tiberius jumped onto her desk she leapt onto her chair.

The children stopped in their tracks. Henrietta tried to grab Tiberius. Tiberius jumped off the desk and ran under the chair. Miss Merryweather shrieked, "help children, help! Get that mouse out of this classroom NOW!"

"No problem," said Tiberius, "I'm off," and with that he scampered outside.

Miss Merryweather looked very flustered as she gingerly stepped off her chair.

The boys and girls were trying not to giggle. They all thought it was great fun.

Tiberius hid outside and waited for school to finish. When Georgina and Henrietta came out, still giggling, Tiberius asked them what all the commotion had been about.

“Well,” said Georgina, “I got the feeling that Miss Merryweather isn’t too keen on mice.”

“Oh, that’s a shame,” said Tiberius, “because I really enjoyed myself. Do you think she would mind if I came again tomorrow?”

What do you think?